ISBN 978-1-333-72145-9
PIBN 10539258

This book is a reproduction of an important historical work. Forgotten Books uses state-of-the-art technology to digitally reconstruct the work, preserving the original format whilst repairing imperfections present in the aged copy. In rare cases, an imperfection in the original, such as a blemish or missing page, may be replicated in our edition. We do, however, repair the vast majority of imperfections successfully; any imperfections that remain are intentionally left to preserve the state of such historical works.

1 MONTH OF
FREE
READING

at
www.ForgottenBooks.com

By purchasing this book you are eligible for one month membership to ForgottenBooks.com, giving you unlimited access to our entire collection of over 700,000 titles via our web site and mobile apps.

To claim your free month visit:
www.forgottenbooks.com/free539258

English
Français
Deutsche
Italiano
Español
Português

www.forgottenbooks.com

Mythology Photography **Fiction**
Fishing Christianity **Art** Cooking
Essays Buddhism Freemasonry
Medicine **Biology** Music **Ancient**
Egypt Evolution Carpentry Physics
Dance Geology **Mathematics** Fitness
Shakespeare **Folklore** Yoga Marketing
Confidence Immortality Biographies
Poetry **Psychology** Witchcraft
Electronics Chemistry History **Law**
Accounting **Philosophy** Anthropology
Alchemy Drama Quantum Mechanics
Atheism Sexual Health **Ancient History**
Entrepreneurship Languages Sport
Paleontology Needlework Islam
Metaphysics Investment Archaeology
Parenting Statistics Criminology
Motivational

Ontario
Library Association.

Catalogue of Children's Books recommended
for Public Libraries. ¡Aníba

Alphabetically arranged by Authors, giving
title, publisher and price.

Compiled by

NORMAN GURD, B.C.L.,
President O.L.A.

C. A. ROWE,
Brockville Public Library.

EFFIE A. SCHMITT,
Berlin Public Library.

1906.

TORONTO:
Printed and Published by L. K. CAMERON, Printer to the King's Most Excellent Majesty.
1906.

Ontario
Library Association.

Catalogue of Children's Books recommended
for Public Libraries.

———

Alphabetically arranged by Authors, giving title, publisher and price.

———

Compiled by

NORMAN GURD, B.C.L.,
President O.L.A.

C. A. ROWE,
Brockville Public Library.

EFFIE A. SCHMITT,
Berlin Public Library.

1906.

WARWICK BRO'S & RUTTER, Limited, Printers
TORONTO

CHILDREN'S BOOKS.

This list has been prepared for Ontario Libraries by a Committee of The Ontario Library Association.

It is intended as a guide for Librarians and Library Boards in the selection of books for children. The name of the Author, title of the book, name of the publisher, and retail price, are given. Library Boards should be allowed a discount from the retail prices. The aim of the Committee has been to recommend such books as shall "cultivate the imagination, broaden the horizon, and add to the stock of knowledge of the child."

The children's section should include good stories, history, biography, travel, science, poetry, and, in fact, books in every department of literature. The children's section is probably the most important in the library. It is a training school for readers. The aim of every librarian is, or should be, to foster amongst the patrons of the library a taste for good literature. Little can be done, however, with the confirmed reader of fiction, but the child who is just beginning to form his taste for reading may be led along the lines of natural inclination to an appreciation of the best in literature.

The child reading nothing but stories of adventure may be induced to take out an interesting book of travel.

Fairy tales are eagerly read by children, and their educational value is now fully recognized. A child who is fond of fairy tales may be introduced to the Greek, Roman and Scandinavian mythologies, without which no one can fully understand the literature of to-day.

The child who is interested in the fabled heroes of myth and legend may easily be led to take an interest in the real heroes of history, especially the great men who founded our country and our Empire.

Macaulay's Lays of Ancient Rome is an excellent first book of poetry for boys, so also is the Lays of the Scottish Cavaliers, as narrative poetry appeals especially to the child. Poems, such as have been mentioned, may be made first rungs in the ladder until the child, step by step, comes to appreciate the works of the world poets.

Most children are fond of Nature books, and the well equipped children's library should contain a good selection of books on natural history.

Stories of invention and elementary science books will be found of interest to many juvenile readers. The English classics and good translations of foreign classics should find place upon the children's shelves. It may be that comparatively few children can be found who appreciate them, but they should be there for those who do. It is advisable to procure handsome illustrated editions of such books, so that they may be as attractive as possible, and the librarian should take special pains to increase their circulation. A child brought into contact with what is best in literature may develop a special taste which may indicate what should be his life-work.

The library should contain a large number of good stories. These will attract the child to the library, and an opportunity is then given to the librarian to recommend better reading.

The library must meet the competition of the dime novel and the sensational story paper, and for this purpose nothing is more effective than the sound wholesome fiction of Henty, Strang or Macdonald Oxley. The librarian should not attempt to force any book on a child. He should take an interest in each child and endeavor to ascertain the child's taste, so that he may tactfully influence the reading of the child for good by easy steps. Frequent additions should be made to the children's section. This is a much better plan than that of making additions only yearly or half yearly Children are much more interested in the library where library's work for children.

This list has not been graded according to the age of the child. All such grading is arbitrary. What is best for a child at a certain age depends on the individuality of the child, and of this the librarian or the teacher is the best judge, having, of course, due regard to the child's own inclination.

One objection to graded lists is that the class is made the unit instead of the child. Many children are able to read and appreciate books far beyond the capacity of some of the adult readers.

Where statistics have been obtained as to the circulation of books among children, it is found that books considered as quite beyond the comprehension of the ordinary child have a very considerable circulation among children. It follows, also, from what has been said that the library should have no age limit, but that any child, no matter how young, desiring a book, should have the privileges of the library.

Where possible the Library Board should provide a special room for children, separate from the general stackroom where children's books can be placed by themselves. Where this is not possible, a section of the stackroom should be set aside for juvenile literature. Free access to the shelves encourages a wider range of reading.

A child who reads nothing but stories may be attracted to a better class of literature while examining the shelves. It is not pretended that the following list is exhaustive or complete, and no doubt there are many sins of omission, but it is hoped that no book is included which upon any grounds should not have been placed on the list.

The annual list of best books issued by The Ontario Library Association includes books for juveniles as well as adults, and should be consulted by librarians.

The Committee has received valuable assistance from a number of publishers, librarians and others, and desire to return its warmest thanks to those who have thus aided it in its work.

NORMAN GURD,

President Ontario Library Association.

Sarnia Public Library, April, 1906.

O. L. A. LIST OF CHILDREN'S BOOKS.

CONTENTS.

(5)

History and Biography

Author.	Title.	Publisher.	Price.
Bain, J. A...............	Nansen....................	Nisbet.......	2s 0d
Baldwin, J	Fifty Famous Stories Re-told	Am. Bk. Co..	$0 35
Baldwin, J	Thirty Famous Stories Re-told........,...........	Am. Bk. Co..	$0 35
Barnes..................	Drake and his Yeomen....................	Macmillan ..	$2 00
Beesley	Stories from History of Rome..................	Macmillan...	$0 35
Besant, Sir W	Story of Alfred the Great...................	Appleton	$0 25
Bevan, A. B...........	Sailor of King George...................	Murray.....	8s 0d
Blaisdell, E F..........	Stories from English History..................	Ginn.	$0 40
Bolton, S..............	Poor Boys who became Famous................	Crowell	$1 50
Bolton, S.............	Girls who became Famous..................	Crowell	$1 50
Bolton, S.............	Famous English Authors	Crowell	$1 50
Bolton, S.............	Famous English Statesmen	Crowell	$1 50
Bolton, S.............	Famous European Artists..................	Crowell	$1 50
Bonner, J	Child's History of France.................	Harper.....	$2 00
Bourne, H. R. F........	Sir Philip Sidney	Putnam......	$1 50
Brooks, E. S...........	True Story of Columbus..................	Lothrop	$1 25
Brooks, E. S...........	Historic Girls..................	Putnam......	$1 50
Butterworth, H. W.....	Magellan	Appleton....	$1 50
Calcott, Lady..........	Little Arthur's History of England............	Copp,Clark ..	$0 55
"A Canuck"	Pen Pictures of Early Pioneer Life in Upper Canada	Briggs.......	$2 00
Church, A. J.........	Stories from English History...................	Macmillan...	$1 25
Clarke, M	Story of Caesar	A. B. Co ...	$0 45
Clement, W. H. P......	History of Canada...................	Briggs	$0 50
Compton, H...........	King's Hussar	Cassell	8s 0d
Creasey, E............	Fifteen Decisive Battles	Macmillan...	$0 70
Cumberland, B	History of the Union Jack..................	Briggs.......	$1 50
Currie, E. A...........	Laura Secord	Briggs......	$1 50
Danby, Paul...........	Red Army Book	Blackie.....	6s 0d
Denison, G. T..........	Soldiering in Canada	Morang	$1 50
Dickens, C.............	Childs' History of England..................	Various ed.	
Duncan, D. M	Story of the Canadian People.................	Morang.....	$0 60
Dunlop, Dr	Recollections of the American War............	Briggs.......	$1 00
Edgar, Lady...........	Ten years of Upper Canada in Peace and War, 1805-15	Briggs......	$1 50
Edgar, J. G...........	Boyhood of Great Men...................	Harper......	$1 00
Edgar, J. G...........	Foot Prints of Famous Men...............	Harper.....	$1 00
Edgar, J. G...........	Sea Kings and Naval Heroes..............	Harper.....	$1 00
Edgar, P	Romance of Canadian History...............	Morang	$0 75
English Men of Action..	Nelson	Macmillan.each	$0 75

Wolfe

Colin Campbell

Gordon

Henry V.

Livingston

Lord Lawrence

Wellington

Dampier

Monk

Stafford

Warren Hastings

Peterborough

Capt. Cook

Sir Henry Havelock

Clive

Author.	Title.	Publisher.	Price.
English Men of Action..	Sir Charles Napier		
	Warwick		
	Drake		
	Rodney		
	Montrose		
	Dundonald		
Farmer, L. H.	Boys' Book of Famous Rulers	Crowell	$1 50
Farmer, L. H.	Girls' Books of Famous Queens	Crowell	$1 50
Finnemore	Boys and Girls of Other Days, 2 vols.	Macmillan.each	$0 40
Finnemore	Men of Renown	Macmillan	$0 35
Finnemore	King Alfred to Lord Roberts	Macmillan	$0 35
Fitchett, W. H.	Fights for the Flag	Bell	$1 25
Fitchett, W. H.	Deeds that Won the Empire	Bell	$1 25
Fitchett, W. H.	Nelson and His Captains	Scribner	$1 50
Fitchett, W. H.	Wellington and His Men	Scribner	$1 50
Fitchett, W. H.	Tale of the Great Mutiny	Scribner.	$1 50
Fitchett, W. H.	Commander of the Hirondelle	Bell	$1 25
Fitchett, W. H.	How England Saved Europe, 4 vols	Bell...each.	$1 25
Fitzgibbon, M.	A Veteran of 1812	Briggs	$1 00
Freeman, E. A.	Old English History for Children	Macmillan	$1 50
Frost, Rev. F.	Sketches of Indian Life	Briggs	$1 50
George, H. R.	Battles of English History	Dodd	$2 00
Gilman, F.	Magna Charta Stories	Blackie	2s 0d
Gomme, G. L.	Kings' Story Book	Longmans	$2 00
Gomme, G. L.	Queens' Story Book	Longmans	$2 00
Gomme, G. L.	Princes' Story Book	Longmans	$2 00
Gomme, G. L.	Princesses' Story Book	Longmans	$2 00
Gordon, A. W.	Recollections of a Highland Subaltern	Arnold	8s 0d
Guerber, H.	Story of the Greeks	Am. B. Co	$0 60
Guerber, H.	Story of the Romans	Am. B. Co	$0 60
Guerber, H.	Story of the English	Am. B. Co	$0 60
Gurney, G.	Girlhood of Queen Victoria	Longmans	$1 75
Haight Conniff	Country Life in Canada Fifty Years Ago	Briggs	$2 00
Hamilton, G.	English Kings in a Nutshell.	Am. B. Co	$0 60
Hardy, E. J	Thomas Atkins	Nelson	4s 0d
Hartley, C. G.	Stories of Early British Heroes	Nelson	4s 6d
Hope, A. R.	Stories of old Renown	Blackie	2s 6d
Hopkins, J. C.	Story of the Dominion	Winston	$2 50
Hulme, F. E	Flags of the World	Warne	$2 00
Jeffry, W	Century of Our Sea Story	Murray	8s 0d
Johonnot, J	Stories of the Olden Times	Am. B. Co	$0 50
Joyce, P. W.	Child's History of Ireland	Longmans	$0 50
Keppel. Sir H.	Sailor's Life under Four Sovereigns, (4 vols.)	Macmillan	24s 0d
King, MacKenzie	Secret of Heroism	Revell	$1 25
Kingsley, R. G	Children of Westminster Abbey	Loth	$1 00
Kirkland	Short History of Italy	McClurg	$1 50
Laing, Mrs.	Heroes of the Seven Hills	Coates	$0 75
Laing, Mrs.	Seven Kings of the Seven Hills	Coates	$0 75
Laing, Mrs.	Conquests of the Seven Hills	Coates	$0 75
Lang, A.	True Story Book	Longmans	$2 00
Lang, A	Red True Story Book	Longmans	$2 00
Leslie, May.	Historical Sketches of Scotland	Bryant	$1 00
Lillie, Lucy	Story of Music	Harper	$0 60
Longmans	Ship Historical Readers	Longmans,ea.	1s 6d
Low, F. H.	Story of Queen Victoria's Dolls	Newnes	$1.25
Lyde.	Age of Drake	Macmillan	$0 40

Author.	Title.	Publisher.	Price.
Strickland, Agnes	True Stories from Modern History	Coates	$0 75
Tappan, E. M	Makers of England Series :—		
	In the Days of Alfred the Great	Lee	$1 00
	In the Days of William the Conqueror	Lee	$1 00
	In the Days of Queen Elizabeth	Lee	$1 00
	In the Days of Queen Victoria	Lee	$1 00
Towle, G. M	Drake the Sea King of Devon	Lee	$1 00
Upton, G. P	Little Dauphin	McClurg	$1 00
Upton, G. P	Frederick the Great	McClurg	$1 00
Upton, G. P	Maria Theresa	McClurg	$1 00
Upton, G. P	Joan of Arc.	McClurg	$1 00
Upton, G. P	William Tell	McClurg	$1 00
Waterloo, S	Story of Ab	Doubleday	$1 50
Weaver, E. P	Builders of the Dominion :—		
	The East	Copp	$0 35
	The West	Copp	$0 35
Weaver, E. P	Canadian History for Boys and Girls	Briggs	$0 50
Wightman, F. A	Our Canadian Heritage	Briggs	$1 00
Wilson, C. D	Story of the Cid	Lee	$1 25
Winthrow, A. H	Popular History of Canada	Briggs	$3 00
Winthrow, A. H	Native Races of North America	Briggs	$0 75
Woods, W. C	Isle of the Massacre	Pub. Synd	$1 25
Yonge, C. M	Prince and Page	Macmillan	$0 70
Yonge, C. M	Book of Golden Deeds	Macmillan	$0 90
Yonge, C. M	Book of Worthies	Macmillan	$0 90
Yonge, C. M	Unknown to History	Macmillan	$0 70
Yonge, C. M	Young Folks History of Greece	Lothrop	$1 00
Yonge, C. M	Young Folks History of Germany	Lothrop	$1 00
Yonge, C. M	Young Folks History of Rome	Lothrop	$1 00
Yonge, C. M	Young Folks History of France	Lothrop	$1 00
Yonge, C. M	Young Folks History of England	Lothrop	$1 00
Young	Stories of the Maple Land	Copp, Clark	$0 25

Travel

Author.	Title.	Publisher.	Price.
Adams, W. D	Round the World with the Union Jack	Ward	4s 0d
Alcott, L. M	Shawl Straps	Roberts	$1 00
Andrews, J	Seven Little Sisters	Ginn	$0 50
Andrews, S	Each and All	Ginn	$0 50
Anson	Voyage Round the World	Blaikie	1s 0d
Ayrton, M. C	Child Life in Japan	Heath	$0 20
Baker, Sir S. W	True Tales for my Grandsons	Macmillan	$1 00
Ballou, M	Due North	Houghton	$1 50
Ballou, M	Due South	Houghton	$1 50
Ballou, M	Foot Prints of Travel	Ginn	$0 60
Blaisdell, E. F	Child Life in Many Lands	Macmillan	$0 40
Bolton, S. K	Famous Voyages	Crowell	$1 50
Boyesen, H. H	Boyhood in Norway	Scribners	$1 25
Brassey, Lady	Round the World in the Sunbeam	Longmans	$0 75
Bullen, F	Cruise of the Cachelot	Briggs	$0 75
Bullen, F	Deep Sea Plunderings	Appleton	$1 50
Bullen, F	Idylls of the Sea	Appleton	$1 25
Campbell, H	My Australian Girlhood	Blackie	$1 50
Carpenter, F. G	Travels Through Asia	Am. Bk. Co.	$0 60
Chance, L. M	Little Folk of Many Lands	Ginn	$0 45
Corbin, J	School Boy Life in England	Harper	$1 25

Author.	Title.	Publisher.	Price.
Corbin, J.	An American at Oxford	Harper	$1 25
Couch, Quiller	Story of the Sea	Cassell	$1 25
Doubleday, R.	Year in a Yawl	Doubleday	$1 25
Du Chaillu, P. B.	Gorilla Country	Harper	$1 00
Du Chaillu, P. B.	Country of Dwarfs	Harper	$1 00
Du Chaillu, P. B.	Land of the Long Night	Scribners	$2 00
Eastman, C. A.	Indian Boyhood	McClure	$1 60
Edgar, Sir Jas.	Canada and its Capital	Morang	$2 50
Famous Discoveries		Blackie	2s 6d
Field, Flood and Forest		Blackie	2s 6d
Frechette, L.	Christmas in French Canada	Morang	$2 00
Froude, J.	English Seamen of the Sixteenth Century	Longmans	$1 50
Geikie, J. C.	Adventures in Canada	Coates	$0 75
Griffis, W. E.	Romance of Discovery	Wilde	$1 50
Graham, E. Maud	A Canadian Girl in South Africa	Briggs	$1 00
Haight, Conniff	A United Empire Loyalist in Great Britain: Here and There in the Home Land	Briggs	$2 25
Hale, E. E.	Stories of Discovery	Little	$1 00
Hale, E. E.	Stories of Adventure	Little	$1 00
Hall, B.	Voyages and Travels	Nelson	$2 00
Headland, I. T.	Chinese Boy and Girl	Revell	$1 00
Herbertson	Africa	Macmillan	$0 65
Herbertson	America (South and Central)	Macmillan	$0 65
Herbertson	Asia	Macmillan	$0 65
Herbertson	Australia and Oceania	Macmillan	$0 65
Herbertson	Europe	Macmillan	$0 65
Hope, A. R.	Young Travellers' Tales	Blackie	2s 6d
Jacobs, J	Wonder Voyages	Macmillan	$1 50
Jones, Jas. Edmund	Camping and Canoeing	Briggs	$0 50
Jenks, Tudor	Boys' Book of Explorations	Doubleday	$2 00
Johnston, W. H.	French Pathfinders of N. A.	Little	$1 50
Johnston, W. H.	World's Discoverers	Little	$1 50
Johnston, W. H.	Pioneer Spaniards of North America	Little	$1 50
Kellog, E. M.	Australia	Silver	$0 50
Keppis, A	Cook's Voyages	Routledge	$1 50
Kingsley, H	Tales of Old Travel	Macmillan	$0 70
Kingston, W. H.	Voyage Round the World	Nelson	$1 25
Kirby, M. E.	Sea and its Wonders	Nelson	$1 75
Knox, T.	Travels of Marco Polo	Putnam	$1 75
Knox, T.	Boy Travellers in Asia	Harper	$3 00
Knox, T.	Boy Travellers in Africa	Harper	$3 00
Knox, T.	Boy Travellers in Australia	Harper	$3 00
Knox, T.	Boy Travellers in Central Europe	Harper	$3 00
Knox, T.	Boy Travellers in Great Britain and Ireland	Harper	$3 00
Knox, T.	Boy Travellers in Northern Europe	Harper	$3 00
Knox, T.	Boy Travellers in Southern Europe	Harper	$3 00
Laughton, J. K.	Sea Fights and Adventures	Allen	6s 0d
Laut, A.	Story of the Trapper	Briggs	$1 50
Laut, A.	Pathfinders of the West	Briggs	$2 00
Laut, A.	Vikings of the Pacific	Briggs	$2 00
Laurie, A	Schoolboys in France	Dana Estes	$1 00
Laurie, A	Schoolboys in Japan	Dana Estes	$1 00
Laurie, A	Schoolboys in Italy	Dana Estes	$1 00
Laurie, A	Schoolboys in Russia	Dana Estes	$1 00
Lee, E	Britain Over the Sea	Morang	$1 00
Lubbock, B	Round the Horn	McClurg	$2 00

Author.	Title.	Publisher.	Price.
Lucas, E. V.	Visit to London	Brentano	$1 50
Lucas, E. V.	Book of Shops	Dutton	$2 50
Lyde	British Isles	Macmillan	$0 40
Lyde	British Empire	Macmillan	$0 40
Lyde	Europe	Macmillan	$0 40
Lyde	Africa	Macmillan	$0 40
Lyde	Asia	Macmillan	$0 40
Lyde	America	Macmillan	$0 40
MacLean	Lone Land Lights	Briggs	$0 35
MacLean	Indians	Briggs	$1 00
MacLean	Canada Savage Folk	Briggs	$2 50
McNaughton, Margaret	Overland to Cariboo	Briggs	$1 00
Macmillan	Geography Readers—		
	British Empire	Macmillan	$0 30
	England and Wales	Macmillan	$0 30
	Colonies of Great Britain	Macmillan	$0 35
	Countries of Europe	Macmillan	$0 35
Martineau	Feats on the Fiords	Blackie	2s 0d
McDougall, J	Path Finding on Plain and Prairie	Briggs	$1 00
McDougall, J	Forest, Lake and Prairie	Briggs	$1 00
McDougall, J	Saddle, Sled and Snow Shoe	Briggs	$1 00
McIntyre, A	Canadian West	Morang	$0 40
Melville, H	Moby Dick	Dana Estes	$1 25
Melville, H	Typee	Heath	$0 45
Miller, O. T.	Little People of Asia	Dutton	$2 50
Morris, M.	Tales of the Spanish Main	Macmillan	$2 00
Morris, C.	Heroes of Discovery in America	Lippincott	$1 25
Murche	Land and Water	Macmillan	$0 35
Murche	World Wide Empire	Macmillan	$0 60
Murche	British Isles	Macmillan	$0 50
Murche	England	Macmillan	$0 45
Murche	Our Earth as a Whole	Morang	$0 60
Oxley, J. McD	Boy Tramps Across Canada	Crowell	$1 25
Oxley, J. McD	Romance of Commerce	Crowell	$1 25
Parkin, Dr.	Round the Empire	Copp	$0 50
Peary, J. D.	Snow Baby	Stokes	$1 30
Peary, R. E.	Snowland Folk	Stokes	$1 25
Perry, F. P.	Japanese Garland	Lothrop	$0 75
Pratt, M. L.	Stories of Australasia	Ed. Pub. Co.	$0 60
Pratt, M. L.	People and Places. 5 vols	Ed. Pub. Co., each	$0 60
Reid, Mayne	Odd People	Routledge	$0 75
Roberts, C. G. D.	Around the Camp Fire	Briggs	$1 25
Slocum, J.	Around the World	Scribner	$0 50
Smith, Goldwin	Trip to England	Briggs	$0 30
Smith, G. B.	Romance of South Pole	Nelson	2s 0d
Spyri, Heidi	Little Swiss Girl	Ginn	$0 40
Spyri, Heidi	Moni	Ginn	$0 40
Starr, F.	Strange Peoples	Heath	$0 40
Starr, F.	American Indians	Heath	$0 45
Stockton, F. B.	Buccaneers and Pirates	Macmillan	$1 50
Stockton, F. B.	Personally Conducted	Scribners	$2 00
Stories of the Sea in Former Days		Blackie	2s 6d
Strange Lands near Home		Ginn	$0 25
Taylor, Bayard	Boys of Other Countries	Putnam	$1 25
Toward the Rising Sun		Ginn	$0 25

Author.	Title.	Publisher.	Price.
Traill, C. P............Lost in the Back Woods.........................Nelson			.....3s 0d
Tyrrell, J. W..........Across the Sub-Arctics of Canada.................Briggs			......$1 50
Under Sunny Skies...Ginn			.......$0 25
Verne, Jules.........:..Great Explorers of 19th Century.................Scribners			....$2 50
Verne, Jules............Great Navigators of 18th Century.................Scribners			....$2 50
Wade, M. H........Ten Little Indians ....Wilde			......$1 00
Wade, M. H...........Little Cousin Series :			
	Little Canadian Cousin ....Page		........$0 60
	Little English Cousin, &c....................Page		........$0 60
Wiggin, K.D. ....Penelope's English Experiences...................Houghton			...$1 00
Wiggin, K. D..........Penelope's Progress (Scotland)...................Houghton			...$1 25
Wiggin, K. D..........Penelope's Irish Experiences....................Houghton			...$1 25
Wide World...Ginn			.......$0 25
Winthrow, W. H......Our Own Country: Canada, Scenic and Descriptive..Briggs			.......$3 00
Yonge, C. M...........Little Lucy's Wonderful Globe...................Macmillan			...$0 50
Young, E. R............On the Indian Trail.........................Revell			.......$1 00
Young, E. R............Three Boys in the Great Lone Land ....Briggs			.......$1 25
Young, E. R............Indian Wigwams................................Briggs			.......$1 25
Young, E. R............By Canoe and Dog Train ....Briggs			......$1 00

Nature.

Author	Title	Publisher	Price
Aaron, Murray..........Butterfly Hunters...............................Scribners			....$1 00
Aiken & Barbauld ......Eyes and no Eyes.:...............................Heath			...... $0 20
Allen, Grant...........Story of the Plants..............................Appleton			....$0 35
Allen, Grant............Flashlights on Nature ....Briggs			.......$1 25
Allen, Grant............In Nature's Workshop...........................Briggs			.......$1 50
Andrews, Jane..........Stories of My Four Friends.....................Ginn			.........$0 50
Andrews, Jane..........Stories Mother Nature Told Her Children.........Ginn			.......$0 50
Andrews, L. F...........Botany All the Year Round.....................Am. Bk. Co.			.$1 00
Andrews, W. R. S......Bob and His Guides.............................Scribners			....$1 50
Atkinson, G. F.........First Studies of Plant Life.......................Copp			......$0 60
Badenoch, L. N.........Romance of the Insect World....................Macmillan			...$0 60
Bailey, F. M..........:..Birds Through an Opera Glass..................Houghton			...$0 75
Bailey, L. H............First Lessons With Plants.........................Macmillan			...$0 40
Bailey, L. H....... ....Botany...Morang			......$1 10
Baker, Sir S. W.. ...:...Wild Beasts.....................................Macmillan			...$3 50
Baldwin, J.............Horse Fair......................................Century			...$1 50
Baskett, J. R..........Story of the Fishes ....:......................Appleton			....$0 75
Bass, M. S.............Plant Life ....Heath			.......$0 25
Bass, M. S.............Animal Life ....Heath			......$0 35
Beal, W. J............Seed Dispersal ....Ginn			.........$0 35
Beale, S. ....Profitable Poultry Keeping ....Judd			.........$1 25
Beard, J. C............Curions Homes.................................Appleton			....$0 65
Bergens, F. D........:..Glimpses of the Plant World ·.................Ginn			........$0 40
Biart, L...............Adventures of a Young Naturalist..............Harper			......$1 25
Bignell, E..............Mr. Chupes and Miss Jenny ....Baker-Taylor.			$1 25
Blanchard, N..........How to Know the Birds........................Briggs			.......$1 35
Blanchard, N ....How to Attract the Birds......................Briggs			.......$1 35
Blanchard, N ....Bird Neighbors ....Briggs			.......$2 00
Blanchard, N ...,.....Birds that Hunt and are Hunted ....Briggs			.......$2 00
Bolton, S..............Our Devoted Friend the Dog....................Page			.......$1 50
Bostock, F. C. ....Training of Wild Animals ....Century			.....$1 00
Brown, J..............Rab and his Friends ....Heath			.......$0 20
Buchanan, H ....True Animal Stories............................Macmillan			...$0 35
Buchanan, H ....Lessons on Country Life.......................Macmillan			...$0 90

Author.	Title.	Publisher.	Price.

Buckland, F ....Curiosities of Natural History, 4 vols ....Macmillan ea$0 70
Bullen, F. G...........Denizens of the Deep...........................Briggs. $1 75
Burroughs, J ....Squirrels and other Fur Bearers.................Houghton ...$1 00
Burroughs, J...........Winter Sunshine..............................Houghton ...$1 00
Burroughs, J...........Wake Robin.. ....Houghton ...$1 00
Burt, M. E. ....Little Nature Studies from Burroughs ....Ginn......·...$0 25
Cecil, E ....Children's Gardens . ...Macmillan. ..$1 50
Chamberlain, Mrs., and C. P. Traill. Canadian Wild Flowers, with plates
   colored by hand, net ....Briggs.......$6 00
Chamberlain, Mrs., and C. P. Traill. Canadian Wild Flowers, uncolored
   plates ....Briggs, net ..$2 50
Chamberlain...........Canadian Birds................................Copp, Clark..$0 30
Chambers, R. W. ......Orchard Land ....Harpers.....$1 50
Chambers, R. W. ......Riverland ....Harpers.....$1 50
Chambers, R. W. ......Forestland...................................Harpers.....$1 50
Chambers, R. W. ......Meadowland..................................Harpers.....$1 50
Champlin, J. D ....Young Folks Cyclopædia of Natural History......Holt $2 50
Chapman, F ....Color Key to N. A. Birds.....................Briggs. $2 50
Clute, W. W...........Our Ferns and their Haunts ....Stokes.......$2 00
Comstock, A. B........Ways of the Six Footed ....Ginn........$0 40
Cones, E ....Citizen Bird ....Macmillan...$1 50
Cram, W. E ....Little Beasts of Field and Wood.................Small $1 25
Crawford, M. R........Guide to Nature Study ....Briggs.......$1 00
Dana...................Plants and Their Children.....................Am. Bk. Co..$0 65
Dickerson, M. C........Moths and Butterflies ....Ginn $1 25
Dale, E. F. ....Story of a Donkey..............................Heath......$0 20
Dale, E. F. ....Crib and Fly ....Heath......$0 20
Drummond, H ....The Monkey who Would Not Kill ....Dodd.......$1 00
DuChailln, P...........The Gorilla Hunters ....Scribners....$2 00
Dugmore, A. R.........Nature and the Camera.......................Briggs......$2 00
Dugmore, A. R.........Bird Homes ....Briggs......$2 00
Dyson, Mrs. W. H .....Stories of the Trees..........................Nelson $1 25
Eastman, C. A.........Red Hunters and the Animal People ....Harper......$1 25
Eddy, S. J............Friends and Helpers ....Ginn........$0 60
Finch, A. V ....Nature Primer ....Ginn........$0 30
Finch, A. V ....Nature Reader ....Ginn........$0 30
Fortescue, J. W. ....Story of the Red Deer ....Macmillan. ..$0 70
Fraser, W. A. ....·. .....Mooswa ....Scribners $1 50
Fraser, W. A. ....Outcasts ....Scribners $1 50
Fraser, W. A. ....Sa Zada Tales.............................Scribners $2 00
Gaiges................. Great World's Farm ....Macmillan. ..$1 00
Gibson, W. H ....Camp Life....·...............................Harper $1 00
Gould, A. W ....Mother Nature's Children ....Ginn........$0 60
Gray, Asa ....Lessons in Botany for Young People ....Am. Bk. Co..$0 60
Haines, W. J. ....Strife of the Sea...............................Barnes $1 60
Hamerton, P. G ....Dogs, Cats and Horses.......................Heath......$0 25
Hardy, A. S ....Hall of Shells................................Appleton $0 60
Haultain, A ....Two Country Walks.........................Morang $1 00
Hemmingway, H. D.....How to make School Gardens ....Doubleday...$1 00
Herrick, S. B ....Earth in Past Ages............................Am. Bk. Co..$0 60
Hickson ....Story of Life in the Seas ....Appleton ...$0 85
Hutchinson............Story of the Hills ....Macmillan...$1 00
Hutton, L ....Boy I knew and Four Dogs ....Harper $1 25
Ingersoll, E............Friends Worth Knowing ....Harper......$1 00
Ingersoll, E............Wild Neighbors.............................Macmillan ...$1 50
Jeffries, R . ...Sir Bevis ....Ginn........$0 30

Author.	Title.	Publisher.	Price.
Johonnot, J	Neighbors with Claws and Hoofs	Am. Bk. Co.	$0 50
Johonnot, J	Neighbors with Wings and Fins	Am. Bk. Co.	$0 40
Lang, A	Animal Story Book	Longmans	$2 00
Lang, A	Red Animal Story Book	Longmans	$2 00
Lindsay	Story of Animal Life	Appleton	$0 35
Linn, W. A	Rob and his Gun	Scribners	$1 00
London, J	Call of the Wild	Morang	$1 50
Long, A. J	Beasts of the Field	Ginn	$0 50
Long, A. J	Fowls of the Air	Ginn	$0 50
Long, A. J	Secrets of the Woods	Ginn	$0 50
Long, A. J	Ways of the Wood Folks	Ginn	$0 50
Long, A. J	Wilderness Ways	Ginn	$0 50
Lounsbery, A	Guide to the Trees	Briggs	$2 50
Lounsbery, A	Guide to Wild Flowers	Briggs	$2 50
Mabie, H. W	Birds Every Child Should Know	Doubleday	$1 00
Martin, M	Yellow Beauty	Laird	$0 50
McIlwraith, T	Birds of Ontario	Briggs	$2 00
Miall, L. C	Round the Year	Macmillan	$0 90
Miller, M. N	Brook Book	Copp, Clark	$1 25
Miller, M. N	Bird Ways	Houghton	$0 60
Miller, O. T	First Book of Birds	Houghton	$1 00
Miller, O. T	Second Book of Birds	Houghton	$1 00
Miller, O. T	Our Home Pets	Harper	$1 25
Morley, M. W	Seed Babies	Ginn	$0 75
Morley, M. W	Flowers and their Friends	Ginn	$0 50
Morley, M. W	Butterflies and Bees	Ginn	$0 60
Morley, M. W	Little Wanderers	Ginn	$0 30
Morley, M. W	Few Familiar Flowers	Ginn	$0 60
Morley, M. W	Insects	Ginn	$0 45
Mulets, L. E	Tree Stories	Copp, Clark	$1 25
Mulets, L. E	Flower Stories	Copp, Clark	$1 25
Mulets, L. E	Bird Stories	Copp, Clark	$1 25
Mulets, L. E	Stories of Little Animals	Copp, Clark	$1 25
Mulets, L. E	Insect Stories	Copp, Clark	$1 25
Mulets, L. E	Stories of Little Fishes	Page	$1 00
Muldrew	Sylvan Ontario	Briggs	$0 75
Murche	Nature Knowledge, 3 vols	Macmillan, ea.	$0 35
Newell, J. H	From Seed to Leaf	Ginn	$0 60
Newell, J. H	Flower to Fruit	Ginn	$0 60
Ollivant, A	Bob, Son of Battle	McClurg	$1 50
Parsons, F. T	How to know the Ferns	Scribners	$1 75
Patterson, S. L	Pussy Meow	Musson	$0 35
Peterson, M. G	How to know the Wild Fruits	Morang	$1 50
Phelps, E. S	Loveliness	Houghton	$1 00
Pierson, C. D	Among the Night People	Copp, Clark	$1 25
Pierson, C. D	Among the Pond People	Copp, Clark	$1 25
Pierson, C. D	Among the Meadow People	Copp, Clark	$1 25
Pierson, C. D	Among the Forest People	Copp, Clark	$1 25
Pierson, C. D	Among the Farm Yard People	Copp, Clark	$1 25
Pratt, M. L	Little Flower Folks, 2 vols., each	E.P. Co	$0 40
Roberts, C. G. D	Kindred of the Wild	Copp	$2 00
Roberts, C. G. D	Watchers of the Trails	Copp	$1 50
Roberts, C. G. D	Red Fox	Briggs	$2 00
Rodway, J	Story of Forest and Stream	Newnes	$0 75
Sandys, E. W	Trapper Jim	Macmillan	$1 50
Sandys, E. W	Sportsman Joe	Macmillan	$1 50

Author.	Title.	Publisher.	Price.
Sanders, M.	Beautiful Joe	Randolph	$0 75
Sanders, M.	Beautiful Joe's Paradise	Page	$1 20
Sanders, M.	Nita	Page	$0 50
Sanders, M.	Princess Sukey	Briggs	$1 25
Savigny, A. G.	Lion the Mastiff	Briggs	$0 75
Schwartz. J. A.	Wilderness Babies	Little	$1 50
Scudder	Frail Children of the Air	Houghton	$1 50
Sears, H.	Fur and Feather Tales	Harper	$1 25
Selous, E.	Romance of Animal Life	Lippincott	$1 50
Sewell, A.	Black Beauty	Rand, McN.	$0 75
Silcox, S.	Modern Nature Study	Morang	$0 75
Skinner, C. M.	Little Gardens	Briggs	$1 25
Smith, F.	Boyhood of a Naturalist	Blackie	3s 6d
Stickney, J. H.	Earth and Sky	Ginn.	$0 35
Stickney, J. H.	Pets and Companions	Ginn.	$0 30
Stickney, J. H.	Bird World	Ginn.	$0 60
Stone & Cram	American Animals	Briggs.	$3 00
Stonehenge	The Dog	Orange, Judd	$1 50
Strong, F. L.	All the Year Round	Ginn.	$0 30
Traill, C. P.	Studies in Plant Life	Briggs	$2 00
Thomson-Seton, E.	Biography of a Grizzly	Copp, Clark.	$1 50
Thomson-Seton, E.	Wild Animals 1 Have Known	Morang	$2 00
Thomson-Seton, E.	Two Little Savages	Briggs	$2 00
Thomson-Seton, E.	Animal Heroes	Briggs	$1 75
Thomson-Seton, E.	Monarch	Morang	$1 25
Thoreau.	Walden	Houghton	$1 00
Torrey.	Every Day Birds	Houghton	$1 00
Van Bruyssel	Population of an Old Pear Tree	Macmillan.	$0 40
Velvin, E.	Rataplan	Altemus.	$1 25
Velvin, E.	Wild Creatures Afield	Altemus.	$1 00
Wagner, R.	Stories from Natural History	Macmillan.	$0 35
Weed, C. M.	Nature Biographies	Copp.	$1 25
Weed, C. M.	Insect Life	Ginn	$0 30
Weed, C. M.	Seed Travellers	Ginn	$0 25
White, S. E.	Magic Forest	Morang.	$1 50
White	Natural History of Selbourne	Morang	$0 50
Wilson	First Nature Reader	Macmillan.	$0 35
Wilson	Second Nature Reader	Macmillan.	$0 35
Wilson	Teachers' Manual Nature	Macmillan.	$0 90
Wood, J.	Natural History	Burt	$0 75
Wood, J.	Wonderful Nests	Longmans	3s 6d
Wood, J.	Strange Dwellings	Longmans	3s 6d
Wright, M. O.	Wabeno	Houghton	$1 50
Wright, M. O.	Tommy Anne	Macmillan	$1 50
Wright, M. O.	Citizen Bird	Macmillan.	$1 50
Wright, M. O.	Four-footed Americans	Macmillan.	$1 50
Wright, M. O.	Story of Plants and Animals	Macmillan.	$0 35
Wright, M. O.	Story of Birds and Beasts	Macmillan.	$0 35
Wright, M. O.	Story of Earth and Sky	Macmillan.	$0 35
Young, E. R.	My Dogs in the Northland	Briggs.	$1 50
Young, E. R.	Hector, my Dog	Briggs.	$1 50

Myths, Legends and Fairy Tales

Author.	Title	Publishers.	Price.
Æsop .	Fables	Macmillan.	$1 00
Anderson, H. C.	Fairy Tales	Macmillan.	$1 25
Anderson, H. C.	Wonder Stories	Houghton	$1 00
Anderson, H. C.	Viking Tales	Houghton	$1 00
Alexander, F.	Hidden Servants	Little	$1 50
Arnold, J. E.	Seven Golden Keys	Blackie	1s 6d
Bain, R. N.	Russian Fairy Tales	Bullen	$1 50
Bain, R. N.	Cossack Fairy Tales	Bullen	$1 50
Bain, R. N.	Turkish Fairy Tales	Bullen	$1 50
Baldwin, J.	Story of Seigfreid	Scribner	$1 50
Baldwin, J.	Story of Roland	Scribner	$1 50
Baldwin, J.	Story of the Golden Age	Scribner	$1 50
Baldwin, J.	Old Greek Stories	Am. Bk. Co.	$0 45
Baldwin, J.	Fairy Tales and Fables	Am. Bk. Co.	$0 35
Baring-Gould	Gettir the Outlaw	Blackie	3s 0d
Baring-Gould	Old English Fairy Tales	Methuen	6s 0d
Brookes, E. S.	Story of King Arthur	Penn	$1 25
Brooks, D.	Stories of the Red Children	Ed. Pub. Co.	$0 40
Brown, A. F.	In the Days of Giants	Houghton	$1 15
Brown, A. F.	Book of Saints and Friendly Beasts	Houghton	$1 25
Brown, A. F.	Flower Princess	Houghton	$1 00
Brown, A- F.	Star Jewels	Houghton	$1 00
Brown, C.	Bold Robin	Dutton	$1 25
Bulfinch	Age of Fable	Crowell	$0 35
Bulfinch	Age of Chivalry	Crowell	$0 35
Bulfinch	Legends of Charlemagne	Crowell	$0 35
Burnett, F. H.	Granny's Wonderful Chair	McClure	$1 25
Burt, M. E.	Herakles of Thebes	Scribner	$0 50
Canton, W.	Reign of King Herla	Dent	$0 50
Carroll, L.	Alice in Wonderland	Macmillan	$0 75
Carroll, L.	Through the Looking Glass	Macmillan	$0 75
Carroll, L.	Sylvie and Bruno	Macmillan	$0 90
Chamisso	Wonderful History of Peter Schlemihl	Ginn	$0 30
Chapin, A. A.	Story of the Rhinegold	Harper	$1 25
Chisholm, L.	Fairyland Tales Told Again	Morang	$2 00
Church, A. J.	Heroes of Chivalry and Romance	Macmillan	$1 75
Church, A. J.	Stories of the Old World	Macmillan	$1 00
Church, A. J.	Stories of the Magicians	Macmillan	$1 00
Church, A. J.	Stories of Charlemagne	Macmillan	$1 75
Collodi, P	Pinocchio	Ginn	$0 40
Crommelin, E. G.	Famous Legends	Century	$1 50
Ewing, J. H.	Flat Iron for a Farthing	Little	$0 50
Firth, E. M.	Stories of Old Greece	Heath	$0 75
Francillon, R. E	Gods and Heroes	Ginn	$0 40
Frere, M	Old Deccan Days	McDonough	$1 25
Frost	Knights of the Round Table	Scribners	$1 50
Frost	Fairies and Folk of Ireland	Scribners	$1 50
Gates, J. S.	Stories of Live Dolls	Bobbs	$1 25
Greene, F. N.	With Spurs of Gold	Little	$1 50
Grimm Bros.	Fairy Tales	Blackie	5s 0d
Harris, J. C.	Uncle Remus	Houghton	$1 50
Harris, J. C.	Nights with Uncle Remus	Houghton	$1 50
Harris, J. C.	Told by Uncle Remus	McClure	$2 00
Hawthorne, N	Wonder Book	Houghton	$1 25

Author.	Title.	Publisher.	Price.
Hawthorne, N	Tanglewood Tales	Houghton	$1 00
Higginson, T. W	Tales of the Enchanted Islands	Macmillan	$1 50
Holbrook, F	Hiawatha Primer	Houghton	$0 75
Ingelow, J	Mopsa the Fairy	Little B	$1 25
Ingelow, J	Three Fairy Stories	Heath	$0 20
Jacobs	Indian Fairy Tales	Nutt	$1 75
Jacobs	Celtic Fairy Tales	Nutt	$1 25
Jacobs	English Fairy Tales	Nutt	$1 25
Judd, M. C	Wigwam Stories	Ginn	$0 85
Keary, A. and E	Heroes of Asgard	Macmillan	$0 50
Kingsley, C	Water Babies	Macmillan	$0 70
Kingsley, C	Greek Heroes	Blackie	2s 0d
Kipling	Just So Stories	Macmillan	$1 50
Kipling	First Jungle Book	Century	$1 50
Kipling	Second Jungle Book	Century	$1 50
Kupfer, G. H	Stories of Long Ago	Heath	$0 35
LaFontaine, J	Fables	Young	$2 50
Lamb, C	Story of Ulysses	Ginn	$0 30
La Moth Foque	Undine and Sintram	Houghton	$1 00
Lang, A	Pink Fairy Book	Longmans	$1 60
Lang, A	Red Fairy Book	Longmans	$1 60
Lang, A	Blue Fairy Book	Longmans	$1 60
Lang, A	Green Fairy Book	Longmans	$1 60
Lang, A	Yellow Fairy Book	Longmans	$1 60
Lang, A	Book of Romance	Longmans	$1 60
Lang, A	Red Book of Romance	Longmans	$1 60.
Lang, A	Arabian Nights	Longmans	$2 00
Lanier,	Knightly Legends of Wales	Scribners	$2 00
Mabie, H. W	Fairy Stories Every Child Should Know	Briggs	$0 90
Mabie, H. W	Myths Every Child Should Know	Briggs	$0 90
Mabie, H. W	Legends Every Child Should Know	Briggs	$0 90
Mabie, H. W	Norse Stories	Briggs	$0 90
MacMillan, M	Tales of Indian Chivalry	Blackie	2s 6d
McDonald, G	At the Back of the North Wind	Routledge	$1 00
McDonald, G	Princess and Curdie	Blackie	3s 6d
McDonald, G	Princess and Goblin	Blackie	3s 6d
McSpadden, J. W	Stories from Wagner	Crowell	$0 60
Mulock, D	Adventures of a Brownie	Macmillan	$0 60
Mulock, D	Fairy Book	Macmillan	$0 90
Murray, A. S	Manual of Mythology	Altemus	$1 25
Nesbit, E	Five Children and It	Dodd	$1 50
Nordau Max	Dwarf's Spectacles	Macmillan	$1 50
O'Shea, M. V	Old World Wonder Stories	Heath	$0 20
Ozaki	Japanese Fairy Book	Dutton	$1 25
Perrault, C	Tales of Passed Times	Dent	$0 50
Porter, J. G	Stars in Song and Legend	Ginn	$0 50
Pyle, H	Robin Hood	Scribner	$3 00
Pyle, H	Story of King Arthur	Scribner	$2 50
Richards, L	Joyous Story of Toto	Little	$1 00
Richards, L	Golden Windows	Little	$1 00
Ruskin, J	King of the Golden River	Ginn	$0 25
Scudder, H. E	Book of Legends	Houghton	$0 50
Scudder, H. E	Book of Folk Stories	Houghton	$0 60
Scudder, H. E	Book of Fables	Houghton	$0 40
Scudder, H. E	Children's Book	Houghton	$2 50
Seper, Countess	French Fairy Tales	Coates	$0 75

2

Author.	Title.	Publisher.	Price.
Singleton, E	Wild Flower Fairy Book	Dodd	$2 00
Smith, E. B	The Book of Nature Myths	Houghton	$0 65
Steele, F. A	Tales of the Punjaub	Macmillan	$1 50
Tappan, E. M	Golden Goose	Houghton	$1 00
Thackery, Wm	Rose and the Ring	Dana	$1 00
Thomson-Seton	Wood Myth and Fable	Briggs	$1 25
Valentine, Mrs.	Old, Old Fairy Tales.	Warne	$1 25
Wiltse, S. E	Folk Lore Stories	Ginn	$0 30
Winnington, Laura	Outlook Fairy Book	Morang	$1 00
Yonge, E. R	Algonquin Indian Tales.	Briggs	$1 50
Zitlaka Sa	Old Indian Legends	Ginn	$0 50

Science

Author.	Title.	Publisher.	Price.
Adams, W. I	Amateur Photography	R.T. Co.	$1 00
Adams	Light Houses	Nelson	$1 25
Andrew, Capt. W. D	Swimming and Life Saving	Briggs	$0 75
Baker, R. S	Boys' Book of Inventions.	McClure	$2 00
Baker, R. S	Boys' Second Book of Inventions	McClure	$2 00
Ball, Sir R. S	Starland	Ginn	$1 00
Barnard, C	First Steps in Electricity	Maynard	$0 60
Beach, D. M	Wonder Stories of Science	Lothrop	$1 00
Beard, D. C	Jack of all Trades	Scribners	$2 00
Beard, L. A. B	Girls' Handy Book	Scribners	$2 00
Beard, L. A. B	Boys' Handy Book	Scribners	$2 00
Binns, C. F	Story of the Potter	Appleton	$0 35
Black, Alex	Captain Kodak	Lothrop	$2 00
Black, Alex	Photography, Indoors and Out	Houghton	$0 75
Blackie	Young Scientists	Blackie	1s 0d
Blackie	Young Chemists	Blackie	1s 6d
Blackie	Young Mechanics	Blackie	1s 4d
Breton, J. M	Canadian Coins.	Author Montreal.	$0 50
Buckley, A. B	Fairy Land of Science	Briggs	$0 75
Buckley, A. B	Through Magic Glasses	Macmillan	$1 50
Carter, A. H	Physical Exercises	Macmillan	$0 90
Chamberlain	How we are Fed.	Macmillan	$0 40
Chamberlain	How we are Clothed	Macmillan	$0 40
Chamberlain	How we are Sheltered	Macmillan	$0 40
Chamberlain	How we are Transported	Macmillan	$0 40
Chambers	Story of the Stars	Appleton	$0 35
Cochrane, R	Wonders of Modern Mechanism	Lippincott	$1 50
Cochrane, R	Romance of Industry and Invention	Chambers	$1 50
Conn, H. W	Story of the Living Machine	Appleton	$0 35
Doubleday	Stories of Inventors	Doubleday	$1 75
Faries, R	Practical Training of Athletes	Outing	$1 00
Gilman, A	Kingdom of Coins	Little	$0 50
Hale, E. E	Stories of Inventors	Little	$1 00
Hall, E. N.	Boy Craftsman	Lothrop	$2 00
Hamilton, J	Our Own and Other Worlds	Briggs	$1 25
Herbertson	Man and His Work	Macmillan	$0 50
Hoffman, Prof	Magic at Home	Cassell	$1 25
Hoffman, Prof	Modern Magic	Routledge	$1 50
Holden, E. S	The Sciences.	Ginn	$0 50
Holden, E, S	Earth and Sky	Appleton	$0 28
Holden, E. S	Stories of the Great Astronomers	Appleton	$0 75
Holden, E. S	Real Things in Nature	Macmillan	$0 65
Homans, J. E	A .B.C. of the Telephone	Audel	$1 00

Author.	Title.	Publisher.	Price.
Hornaday, W. T	Taxidermy	Scribners	$2 00
James, A. R	Girls' Physical Training	Macmillan	$2 00
Johnson, R	Phaeton Rogers	Scribner	$1 50
Kelley, J. G	Boy Mineral Collectors	Lippincott	$1 50
Kelley, L. E	300 Things a Bright Girl Can Do	Estes	$1 20
Kingsley, C	Madam How and Lady Why	Macmillan	$0 70
Martin, E. A	Story of a Piece of Coal	Appleton	$0 35
Meadowcraft, W. H	A.B.C. of Electricity	Empire	$0 50
Moffett, C	Careers of Daring and Danger	Century	$1 80
Munro	Story of Electricity	Appleton	$0 40
Murche, V. T	Science Readers, 6 vols	Macmillan ea. 25c	$0 40
Mussett, De A	Mr. Wind and Madam Rain	Putnam	$2 00
Ogilvie, W. T	Postage Stamps	Sonnenschein	$0 25
Pepper, J. H	Boys' Book of Science	Routledge	$1 50
Pepper, J. H	Boys' Book of Metals	Routledge	$1 50
Pouchet, F. T	The Universe	Blackie	7s 6d
Proctor, Mary	Stories of Starland	Morang	$0 75
Roth, F	First Book of Forestry	Ginn	$0 75
Santos, Dumont A	My Air Ships	Century	$1 40
Scientific American Boy		Munn & Co.	$2 00
Scott Co	Postage Stamps	Scott Co	$0 25
Seely	Story of the Earth	Appleton	$0 35
Serviss, Garret	Astronomy with an Opera Glass	Appleton	$1 50
Shaler, N. S	First Book in Geology	Heath	$0 45
Sloane, G. O	Electric Toy Making	Henley	$1 00
Sloane, G. O	Electricity Simplified	Henley	$1 00
Sloane, G. O	How to Become an Electrician	Henley	$1 00
Sontag, H	Magic Ring of Music	Dent	2s 6d
Stephens, W. P	Canoe and Boat Building	Forest	$2 00
Storey, A. T	Story of Photography	Appleton	$0 35
St. John, M. T	How Two Boys Made Their Own Electrical Apparatus	Scribner	$1 00
Taylor, C. M	Why my Photos are Bad	Jacobs	$1 00
Towle, G. M	Heroes and Martyr's of Invention	Lee	$1 00
Trowbridge	Electrical Boy	Little	$1 50
Trowbridge	Three Boys in an Electrical Boat	Houghton	$1 00
Von Bergen, W	Rare Coins	Author Boston	$0 50
Waite, H. R	Boys' Work Shop	Sonnenschein	$0 50
Wallace, A. R	Wonderful Century	Dodd	$2 50
Wiggin, K. D	Kindergarten	Houghton	$1 00
Williams	Romance of Modern Invention	Briggs	$1 50
Williams	Romance of Modern Engineering	Briggs	$1 50
Williams	Romance of Modern Steam Locomotion	Briggs	$1 50
Wood	How the Worker is Paid	Macmillan	$0 50
Wright, C. H	Childrens' Stories of Great Scientists	Scribner	$1 25

Literature

Alexander, W. J	Anthology of English Poetry	Copp	$0 50
Auger, A	Tennyson for the Young	Macmillan	$0 35
Ariosto's	Stories for Children	Little	$1 00
Aytoun	Lays of the Scottish Cavaliers	Nelson	4s 0d
Baring-Gould, S	Book of Nursery Songs	Methuen	6s 0d
Barham, R. H	Ingoldsby Legends	Macmillan	$0 70
Bates, K	English History told by English Poets	Macmillan	$0 70
Beeching, H. C	Book of Christmas Verse	Methuen	3s 6d
Bell, M	Fairy Tale Plays	McClurg	$1 00

Campbell, William Wilfred	Poems	Briggs	$1 50
Campbell, Chas.	Canada, Metrical Story	Briggs	$0 25
Carmen, Bliss	Ballads of Lost Haven	Page	$1 25
Carmen, Bliss	Behind the Arras	Briggs	$1 50
Carey, Alice & Phoebe	Ballads for Little Folk	Houghton	$1 50
Chesson, N	Tales from Tennyson	Tuck	$1 25
Chesson, N	Tales from Shakespeare	Tuck	$1 25
Chesson, N	Stories from Dante	Warne	$1 25
Church, A. J.	Story of the Illiad	Macmillan	$1 00
Church, A. J.	Story of the Odyssey	Macmillan	$1 00
Church, A. J.	Stories from Homer	Macmillan	$1 25
Church, A. J.	Stories from Livy	Dodd	$1 00
Church, A. J.	Stories from Virgil	Dodd	$1 25
Clarke, M. C	Girlhood of Shakespeare's Heroines	Scribner	$3 00
Cookson, C.	English Poetry for Schools, 2 vols	Macmillan	35c & $0 60
Crawford, Isabel Valancey	Poems	Briggs	$1 50
Crockett, S. R.	Red Cap Tales from Scott	Morang	$2 00
Cunliff, J. W.	Nineteenth Century Literature	Morang	$0 50
Edgar, J. D.	This Canada of Ours	Briggs	$0 50
Field, E.	Little Book of Profitable Tales	Briggs	$1 25
Field, E.	Lullaby Land	Morang	$1 25
Field, E.	Love Songs of Childhood	Scribner	$1 00
Fitzgerald, S. J.	Stories of Famous Songs	McClurg	$3 00
Garrison	Good Night Poetry	Ginn	$0 60
Gibbs, L. R.	Coleridge's Ancient Mariner	Ginn	$0 20
Globe	Poetry Reader	Macmillan	$0 35
Globe	Poetry Books, 4 vols.	Macmillan	15 to 30c
Globe	Readers, 6 vols.	Macmillan	10 to 40c
Graham, K.	Golden Age	Lane	$1 00
Graham, K.	Dream Days	Lane	$1 00
Hale, E. E.	Stories from Baron Munchausen	Heath	$0 20
Haweis, Mrs.	Chaucer for Children	Scribner	$1 25
Henley, W. C.	Lyra Heroica	Scribner	$1 25
Hoffman, A.	Shakespeare's Plays, retold for children, 8 vols.	Dent, each	1s 0d
Hoyts, D. L.	World's Painters.	Ginn	$1 25
Hugo, Victor	Gavroche	Coates	$0 75
Hurll, E. M.	Child Life in Art	Houghton	$0 40
Hurll, E. M.	Riverside Art Series :—		
	Raphael	Houghton	$0 40
	Michael Angelo	Houghton	$0 40
	Van Dyck, etc.	Houghton	$0 40
Ingpen, R.	One Thousand Poems for Children	Hutchinson	$1 50

Author.	Title.	Publisher.	Price.
Jenkins, R. S.	Poems of the New Century	Briggs	$1 00
Jerrold, D.	Fireside Saints	Blackie	2s 6d
Johnson, E. Pauline	Canadian Born	Morang	$0 75
Kipling	Reader	Macmillan	$0 40
Knowles, F. L.	Famous Children of Literature Series :—		
	Little Paul from Dickens	Dana	$0 60
	Little Peter from Maryatt	Dana	$0 60
	Little Nell from Dickens	Dana	$0 60
	Little Eva from Stowe	Dana	$0 60
	Tom and Maggie from Eliot	Dana	$0 60
	Little David from Dickens	Dana	$0 60
Lamb, C. and M.	Tales from Shakespeare	Macmillan	$0 90
Lamb, C.	Poetry for Children	Dent	2s 6d
Lamb, C.	Stories for Children	Dent	3s 6d
Lampman, A.	Poems	Morang	$2 00
Lang, A.	Iliad	Longmans	$1 60
Lang, A.	Odyssey	Longmans	$1 60
Lang, A.	Blue Poetry Book	Longmans	$1 60
Lang, A.	Nursery Rhyme Book	Warne	$2 00
Laugbridge, F.	Ballads of the Brave	Methuen	2s 6d
Lanier S.	Boy's Percy	Scribner	$2 00
Lanier, S.	Boy's Malory's King Arthur	Scribner	$2 00
Lear, E.	Nonsense Book	Little	$2 00
Lighthall, W. D.	Songs of the Great Dominion	Scott	$1 50
Litchfield, M. F.	Five English Poets	Ginn	$0 20
Lochart, J. G.	Spanish Ballads	Putnam	$1 00
Lucas, E. V.	Book of Verses for Children	Grant Richards	6s 0d
Macaulay, Lord	Lays of Ancient Rome	Putnam	$0 50
Mackay, Isabel E.	Between the Lights	Briggs	$0 75
Machar, A.	Lays of the True North	Stock	4s 0d
MacMurchy, Arch	Canadian Literature	Briggs	$1 00
MacLeod M.	Shakespeare Story Book	Gardner	6s 0d
MacLeod, M.	Stories from the Fairie Queen	Gardner	6s 0d
Miller, John	Books: A Guide to Good Reading	Briggs	$0 50
Mitchell, D. G.	About Old Story Tellers	Scribner	$1 25
Montgomery, D. H.	Goldsmith's Vicar of Wakefield	Ginn	$0 30
Montgomery, D. H.	Johnson's Rasselas	Ginn	$0 35
Newbolt, H.	Admirals All	Lane	$0 50
Nicholson, S. H.	British Songs for British Boys	Macmillan	$0 35
Palgrave, F.	Children's Treasury	Macmillan	$0 90
Palmer	Stories from Classic Literature	Macmillan	$1 25
Parry, Judge	Don Quixote for Children	Blackie	6s 0d
Patmore, C	Children's Garland	Macmillan	$0 90
Perry, W. C	Boy's Odyssey	Macmillan	$1 50
Perry, W. C	Boy's Iliad	Macmillan	$1 50
Rabelais, F	Three Good Giants	Houghton	$1
Rand, Dr.	Treasury of Canadian Verse	Briggs	$1
Rand, Dr.	At Minas Basin and Other Poems	Briggs	$1
Richardson	Stories from Old English Poetry	Houghton	$0 70
Rives, H. E.	Tales from Dickens	Bobbs	$1 00
Ruskin, John	Sesame and Lillies (various editions)		
Roberts, Chas. G. D.	Songs of the Common Day	Briggs	$1 25
Sands, G	Master Mosaic Workers	Dent	1s 6d
Scott, Fred George	My Lattice, and other Poems	Briggs	$0 75
Scott, Fred George	The Unnamed Lake	Briggs	$0 75

Shakespeare ....Shakespeare Plays ....Various ed.
Singleton, E............Famous Paintings............................Dodd $1 60
Sprague, H. B..........Milton's Paradise Lost ....Ginn $0 30
Stanley, L..............Patriotic Songs..................................Briggs.......$1 50
Stevenson, R. L........Child's Garden of Verse ....Briggs.......$0 75
Stevenson, R. L........Ballads ....Scribner $1 50
Sweetser, K.............Ten Girls from Dickens.........................Fox Duffield.$1 25
Swift, Dean.............Gulliver's Travels..............................Ginn $0 35
Tappan, E. M..........Old Ballads in Prose ....Houghton ...$1 10
Temple, A. G..........English History Pictured by Painters ....Newnes 10s 6d
Tennyson ....Poems..Various ed.
Towry, H...............Spencer for Children ....Scribner.....$1 25
Warner, C. D..........Being a Boy ....Houghton ...$1 25
Wells, C................Jingle Book ....Macmillan...$1 00
Wetherell, J. E........Poems of the Love of Country.................Morang......$0 75
White, J. S.............Plutarch for Boys..............................Putnam $1 75
White, A. H............Irving's Alhambra ....Ginn $0 40
Wiltse, S. E............Hugo's Jean Valjean ....Ginn $0 90
Witham, R. H.........Elliot's Silas Marner ....Ginn $0 30
Woods, M. A..........Children's Stories in English Literature, 2 vols....Scribner $1 25
Yonge, C. M...........Scott's Ivanhoe................................Ginn $0 60
Yonge, C. M...........Scott's Guy Mannering.........................Ginn $0 60
Yonge, C. M...........Scott's Quenten Durward.......................Ginn $0 60
Yonge, C. M...........Scott's Rob Roy ....Ginn $0 60

Religion and Ethics

Baldwin, J..............Old Stories of the East ....Am. Bk. C...$0 45
Beale, S. H............Stories from the Old Testament.................Stone $1 50
Bible for Children ....Century $3 00
Brown, A. F...........In the Days of the Saints..................... .... Houghton ..$1 00
Bunyan, J ....Pilgrim's Progress..............................Century $1 50
Burdette, R. J.........Before He is Twenty ....Ward $0 75
Canton, Wm...........Child's Book of Saints ....Dent 3s 6d
Chenowith, C..........Stories of the Saints..........................Houghton ...$1 00
Chester, Eliza ....Girls and Women.............................Houghton ...$1 00
Church, A..J..........Stories from the Bible, 2 vols ....Macmillan...$2 50
Conwell, J. A..........Manhood's Morning............................Briggs......$1 00
Cragen, L. E...........Kindergarten Bible Stories ....Revell.......$1 25
Ellis, E. S.............Young Peoples Imitation of Christ.............McClurg.....$1 00
Foster, C. ....Story of the Bible.............................Baker $1 00
Gatty, Mrs. ....Parables from Nature, 2 vols...................Macmillan...$1 50
Guerber, H. A.........Story of the Chosen People....................Am. Bk. Co..$0 60
Hale, E. E.............How to Do It......................Little $1 00
Hofer ....Child's Christ Tales............................Harley $1 00
Houghton, L. S........Telling Bible Stories...........................Scribner.....$1 25
Hurll, E. M...........Bible Beautiful................................Page $2 00
Jackson, H............Bits of Talk for Young Folks...................Little $1 00
Kirkland, E. S..........Speech and Manners ....McClurg ...$0 75
Moulton ....Old Testament Stories.........................Macmillan...$0 50
Moulton ....New Testament Stories ....Macmillan...$0 50
Norton, H. E..........Book of Courtesy ....Macmillan...$0 70
O'Hara, F. C. T.......Snap Shots from Boy Life......................Briggs......$0 75
Sangster, M. E.........That Sweet Story of Old......................McClurg.....$1 25
Smiles, S..............Self Help ....Burt $1 00
Smiles, S..............Character ....Burt $1 00
Smiles, S..............Duty ....Burt $1 00

Author.	Title.	Publisher.	Price.
Smiles, S..............	Thrift..	Burt........	$1 00
Stanley, Dean..........	Sermons for Children...........................	Scribners....	$0 75
Tappan, E. M..........	Christ Story	McClurg.....	$1 50
Walker, W. W.........	Plain Talks on Health and Morals..............	Briggs.......	$0 75
Watson, A. D..........	The Sovereignty of Character..................	Briggs	$1 00
Yonge, C. M...........	Young Folks Bible History.....................	Lothrop.....	$1 00

Games, etc.

Cassels	Book of Sports..................................	Cassell	$1 00
Champlin, J. D........	Cyclopædia of Games and Sports................	Holt........	$2 50
Butter, S. J............	Conundrums and Games.......................	Hausauer....	$0 40
Games Book...............	....	Dutton	$2 00
Hoffman, M. F.........	Games for Everybody...........................	Dodge.......	$0 50
Keene, J. H	Boys' own Guide to Fishing	Lee	$1 50
Little Cook Book for a Little Girl............................		Dana Estes ..	$0 75
Lucas, E. V	What Shall we Do Now?.......................	Grant Richards.6s. 0d
Nugent, M..............	New Games......................................	Doubleday...	$1 50
Outdoor Handy Book		Scribner.....	$2 00
Smedley, V. J	New Games......................................	Doubleday...	$1 50
Stevens, A. W	Practical Rowing................................	Little.......	$1 00
Stuart, R. M..........	Shadow Pictures	Century	$1 00
Thompson, Maurice.....	Boys' Book of Sports...........................	Century	$2 00
White, Mary...........	Child's Rainy Day Book.......................	Doubleday...	$1 10

Stories

Adam and Wethrell.....	An Algonquin Maiden..........................	Briggs.......	$1 50
Alcott, L. M...........	Little Men.....................................	Little Brown.	$1 50
Alcott, L. M...........	Little Women..................................	Little Brown.	$1 50
Alcott, L. M	Eight Cousins..................................	Little Brown.	$1 50
Alcott, L. M...........	Under the Lilacs..............................	Little Brown.	$1 50
Alden, W. L...........	Jimmy Brown	Harper	$0 60
Alden, W. L...........	Cruise of the Ghost............................	Harper	$0 60
Alden, W. L.	Moral Pirates..................................	Harper	$0 60
Aldrich. T. B..........	Story of a Bad Boy............................	Houghton ...	$1 25
Amicis, de E	Heart	Crowell	$1 00
Armstrong, F..........	A Girl's Loyalty	Blackie	3s 6d
Atkinson, J. C.........	Play Hours and Half Holidays..................	Macmillan .	$0 75
Austin, Jane...........	Dora Darling..................................	Lee & Shepard	$1 00
Baker, Sir S	Cast Up by the Sea............................	Harper	$1 25
Ballantyne, R. M.......	Ungava...	Nisbet.......	$1 50
Ballantyne, R. M.......	Settler and Savage.............................	Nisbet.......	$1 50
Ballantyne. R. M.......	Buffalo Runners	Nisbet......	$1 50
Ballantyne, R. M......	Norseman in the West..........................	Nisbet......	$1 50
Barrie, J. M...........	Little White Bird.............................	Copp.......	$1 50
Barr, R.................	Over the Border	Briggs	$1 25
Barr, R.................	In the Midst of Alarms........................	Briggs......	$1.25
Baring-Gould, H........	My Prague Pig.................................	Skeffington ..	1s 0d
Bell, J. J.............	Wee MacGregor	Morang.....	$0 50
Bell, Lillian	Book of Girls	Page........	$1 00
Bennett, John	Barnaby Lee...................................	Copp.......	$1 25
Bennett, John	Master Skylark	Century	$1 50
Black, Wm.............	Four Macnichols	Harper......	$0 60
Blackmore, R. D........	Lorna Doone...................................	Harper......	$1 25
Brerton, Capt..........	Foes of the Red Cockade	Briggs & Copp	$1 50
Brerton, Capt..........	In the King's Service..........................	Briggs & Copp	$1 50
Brerton, Capt..........	With Rifle and Bayonet........................	Briggs & Copp	$1 50

Author.	Title.	Publisher.	Price.
Dickens, C	David Copperfield	Macmillan	$1 00
Dickens, C	Old Curiosity Shop	Macmillan	$0 70
Dickens, C	Christmas Stories	Macmillan	$1 00
Dickson, Mrs. W. J	Miss Dixie ; A Romance of the Provinces	Briggs	$0 50
Dodge, M. M	Hans Brinker	Scribners	$1 50
Doudney, S	Stepping Stones	various editions.	
Doudney, S	Michaelmas Daisy	"	
Doudney, S	When we were Girls Together	"	
Doudney, S	Prudence Winterburn	"	
Doyle, A. C	The Refugees	Harpers	$1 50
Doyle, A. C	Sir Nigel	Harpers	$1 50
Doyle, A. C	White Company	Harpers	$1 50
Doyle, A. C	Micah Clark	Harpers	$1 50
Dryden, Mrs. S. H	Daisy Dryden	Briggs	$1 00
Du Chaillu, P	Lost in the Jungle	Harpers	$1 00
Dumas	Count of Monte Cristo	Various editions.	
Duncan, N	Way of the Sea	Revell	$1 50
Duncan, N	Dr. Luke of the Labrador	Revell	$1 50
Edgeworth, Maria	Moral Tales	Routledge	$1 00
Edgeworth, Maria	Popular Tales	Routledge	$1 00
Edgeworth, Maria	Early Lessons	Routledge	$1 00
Edgeworth, Maria	Parents Assistant	Routledge	$1 00
Eggleston, E	Hoosier School Boy	Briggs	$0 50
Eliot, G	Mill on the Floss	Various editions.	
Everett-Green, E	Gordon Highlander	Nelson	$0 75
Everett-Green, E	Clerk of Oxford	Nelson	$0 75
Everett-Green, E	Golden Gwendolyn	Hutchinson	$1 00
Everett-Green, E	Namesakes	Hutchinson	$1 00
Everett-Green, E	Secret of the Old House	Blackie	2s 6d
Everett-Green, E	Miss Marjorie of Silver Mead	Jacobs	$1 00
Ewing, J. H	Mary's Meadow	Little	$0 50
Ewing, J. H	Six to Sixteen	Little	$0 50
Ewing, J. H	Jackanapes	Little	$0 50
Ewing, J. H	Lob Lie by the Fire	Little	$0 50
Ewing, J. H	Story of a Short Life	Little	$0 50
Fairstar, Mrs	Memoirs of a London Doll	Brentano	$1 25
Farrar, Dean	Eric	Macmillan	$1 00
Farrar, Dean	St. Winnifreds	Macmillan	$1 00
Farrar, Dean	Julian Home	Macmillan	$1 00
Favenc, E	Marooned on Australia	Blackie	2s 0d
Fenn, G. M	Devon Boys	Blackie	3s 6d
Fenn, G. M	In the King's Name	Blackie	3s 6d
Fenn, G. M	Brownsmith's Boy	Blackie	3s 6d
Fenn, G. M	Fixed Bayonets	Blackie	3s 6d
Fenn, G. M	First in the Field	Blackie	3s 6d
Fenn, G. M	Wildwoods life	Blackie	3s 6d
Fenn, G. M	Begumbah	Blackie	3s 6d
Fenn, G. M	Kopje Garrison	Blackie	3s 6d
Ferres, A	His First Kangaroo	Blackie	3s 6d
Finn	That Foot-Ball Game	Fr.Pustet&Co	$0 85
Finn	Tom Playfair	Fr.Pustet&Co	$0 85
Finn	His First and Last Appearance	Fr.Pustet&Co	$0 85
Fletcher, J. S	In the Days of Drake	Blackie	2s 0d
Fletcher, M	Jefferson Junior	Blackie	3s 6d
Fletcher, M	Every Inch a Briton	Blackie	3s 60
Fletcher, R. H	Marjorie and her Papa	Century	$1 0d

26

Author.	Title.	Publisher.	Price.
Fortescue, Hon. J. W.	Drummers Coat	Macmillan	$1 50
Frith, H	Search for the Talisman	Blackie	2s 6d
Gethen, H. F'	Nell's School-days	Blackie	2s 6d
Gibbon, F. P	The Disputed V.C	Blackie	5s 0d
Glanville, E	In Search of the O Kapi	Blackie	6s 0d
Glanville, E	Diamond Seekers	Blackie	6s 0d
Golschmann, L	Boy Crusoes	Blackie	3s 6d
Golschmann, L	Adventures of a Siberian Cub	Page	$1 00
Green, Hon. Mrs	Phantom Picture	Nelson	6s 0d
Green, Hon. Mrs	Grey House on the Hill	Nelson	6s 0d
Greenaway, K	Marigold Garden	Routledge	$2 00
Greenaway, K	Under the Windows	Warne	$1 50
Grenfell, W. T	Harvest of the Sea	Revell	$1 00
Habberton, J	Helen's Babies	Caldwell	$1 50
Habberton, J	Grown up Babies	Caldwell	$1 50
Habberton, J	Who was Paul Grayson?	Caldwell	$1 50
Haggard, H. R	Eric Bright Eyes	Longmans	$1 25
Haggard, H. R	King Solomon's Mines	Longmans	$1 25
Hall, E. K'	That Examination Paper	Blackie	1s 6d
Hamblen, H. E	We Win	Scribners	1 50
Hamerton, P. G	Harry Blount	Little	$1 25
Happyman, H	Box of Stories	Blackie	2s 6d
Harraden, B	Things Will Take a Turn	Blackie	2s 6d
Harrison, F	Boys of Wynport College	Blackie	3s 0d
Hayes, M. J	Prince Lazybones	Harper	$0 60
Hayes, M. J	Princess Idleways	Harper	$0 60
Haynes, H	Clevely Sahib	Nelson	3s 6d
Haynes, H	Under the Lone Star	Nelson	3s 6d
Heddle, E. F	The Towns Verdict	Blackie	6s 0d
Henham, E. G	Menotah		
Henty, G. A.	By England's Aid	Briggs	$0 50
Henty, G. A.	Hold Fast for England	Briggs	$0 50
Henty, G. A.	Red Skin and Cowboy	Briggs	$0 50
Henty, G. A.	With Wolfe in Canada	Briggs	$0 50
Henty, G. A.	With Roberts to Pretoria	Blackie	6s 0d
Henty, G. A.	St. George for England	Briggs	$0 50
Henty, G. A.	Bonnie Prince Charlie	Briggs	$0 50
Henty, G. A.	By Pike and Dike	Briggs	$0 50
Henty, G. A.	By Right of Conquest	Briggs	$0 50
Hickman, W. A	Sacrifice of the Shannon	Briggs	$1 25
Hofmann, H	Slovenly Peter	Coates	$1 50
Hope, A. R	Stories Out of Schooltime	Macmillan	1 00
Howells, W. D	Flight of Pony Baker	Harper	$0 75
Hughes, T	Tom Brown's School Days	Morang / Macmillan	$1 50 / $0 70
Huntington, H. S	His Majesty's Sloop Diamond Rock	Houghton	$1 50
Hyne, C. J. C	Captured Cruiser	Blackie	3s 6d
Hyne, C. J. C	Stimson's Reef	Blackie	2s 6d
Ingelow, Jean	Spinning Wheel Stories	Little	$1 25
Ingelow, Jean	Studies for Stories	Little	$1 25
Ingelow, Jean	Stories Told to a Child	Little	$1 25
Ingelow, Jean	Golden Opportunity	Little	$0 50
Ingelow, Jean	A Sister's Bye-Hours	Little	$1 25
Jacoberns, R	The New Pupil	Macmillan	2s 6d
Jack, A. L	Little Organist of St. Jerome	Briggs	$0 75
Jackson, H. H	Nelly's Silvermine	Little	$1 50

Author.	Title.	Publisher.	Price.
Janvier	Aztec Treasure House	Harper	$1 50
Janvier	In the Sargasso Sea	Harper	$1 25
Jewett, S. O.	Betty Leicester	Houghton	$1 50
Johnston, W.	Tom Graham, V. C	Nelson	3s 6d
Johnston, Mrs. C	Her College Days	Penn	$1 25
Johnson, R.	End of a Rainbow	Scribners	$1 50
Johnson, R.	Phæton Rogers	Scribners	$1 50
Keary, A.	York and Lancaster Rose	Macmillan	$1 00
Kerr, D	Lost City	Harper	$0 60
Kerr, D	Into Unknown Seas	Harper	$0 60
Kingsley, C	Westward Ho	Macmillan	$0 70
Kingsley, C	Hereward the Wake	Macmillan	$0 70
Kingsley, W.	Hillyars and Burtons	Macmillan	$1 00
Kingston, W. H. G.	Young Rajah	Nelson	6s 0d
Kingston, W. H. G.	In the Wilds of Africa	Nelson	6s 0d
Kingston, W. H. G.	Dick Chevely	Nelson	6s 0d
Kingston, W. H. G.	Three Midshipmen	Nelson	6s 0d
Kipling, R	Stalky & Co	Doubleday, Page.	$1 50
Kipling, R	Kim	Doubleday, Page.	$1 50
Kipling, R	Captains Courageous	Century	$1 50
Kipling, R	His Majesty the King	Dana Estes	$0 50
Kirby	Golden Dog	Briggs	$1 25
Kirkpatrick, E. S.	Tales of the St. John	Briggs	$0 75
Laing, Leslie	Queen of the Daffodils	Blackie	2s 0d
LeFeuvre, Amy	His Big Opportunity	R. T. S.	1s 0d
LeFeuvre, Amy	Probable Sons	R. T. S.	1s 0d
LeFeuvre, Amy	Sea Between	R. T. S.	1s 0d
Leighton, R	Golden Galleon	Scribners	$1 50
Leighton, R	Pilots of Pomona	Scribners	$1 50
Leighton, R	Thirsty Sword	Scribners	$1 50
Leighton, R	Wreck of the Golden Fleece	Scribners	$1 50
Liljencrantz, O. L.	Vineland Champions	Appleton	$1 50
Lillie, L. C	Household of Glen Holly	Harper	$0 60
Lillie, L. C	Nan	Harper	$0 60
Lillie, L. C	Rolf House	Harper	$0 60
Lytton, Lord	Harold	Routledge	$1 50
Lytton, Lord	Last of the Barons	Routledge	$1 50
Macdonald, G	A Rough Shaking	Blackie	3s 6d
Macdonald, G	Gutta Percha Willie	Blackie	2s 0d
Macdonald, G	Ronald Bannerman's Boyhood	Blackie	3s 6d
Macdonald, M. P.	Trefoil		
Machar, A.	Marjorie's Canadian Winter	Briggs	$1 00
Machar, A.	Quest of the Fatal River	Lothrop	$1 00
Machar, A.	Donald Graham Knight	Briggs	$1 00
Maclaren, Ian	Young Barbarians	Copp	$1 50
Maclean, John	Warden of the Plains	Briggs	$1 25
Macleod, Mrs, E. S.	Donalda and Cousin Esme	Briggs	$1 00
March, C.	Don's High School Days	Blackie	1s 6d
Marchant, B.	A Heroine of the Sea	Blackie	3s 6d
Martin, Mrs. H.	Bonnie Leslie	Griffith	3s 6d
Martin, Mrs. H.	A Country Mouse	Griffith	3s 6d
Martin, Mrs. H.	Guide, Philosopher and Friend	Griffith	3s 6d
Martineau, H.	Crofton Boys	Routledge	$0 75
Martineau, H.	Peasant and Prince	Routledge	$1 25
Maryatt, Capt	Japhet in Search of a Father	Macmillan	$0 70
Maryatt, Capt	Peter Simple	Macmillan	$0 70

Author.	Title.	Publisher.	Price.
Pickering, E.	A Stout English Bowman	Blackie	3s 6d
Plympton, A. G.	Dear Daughter Dorothy	Little	$1 00
Plympton, A. G.	Little Olive	Little	$1 00
Pollard, E. F.	Lady Isabel	Blackie	2s 6d
Pollard, E. F.	For the Red Rose	Blackie	2s 6d
Pollard, E. F.	White Standard	Blackie	2s 6d
Porter, J.	Thaddeus of Warsaw	Winston	$0 75
Ray, E. C.	Teddy Her Book	Little, Brown.	$1 25
Read, T. B.	Kilgorman	R. T. S.	$1 25
Read, T. B.	Fifth Form at St. Dominics	R. T. S.	$1 25
Read, T. B.	My Friend Smith	R. T. S.	$1 25
Read, T. B.	Dog with a Bad Name	R. T. S.	$1 25
Read, T. B.	Cock House at Tellsgarth	R. T. S.	$1 25
Read, T. B.	Tom, Dick and Harry	R. T. S.	$1 25
Read, T. B.	Three Guinea Watch	R. T. S.	$1 25
Read, T. B.	Reginald Cruden	R. T. S.	$1 25
Reid, M.	Tiger Hunters	Routledge	$0 70
Reid, M.	Headless Horseman	Routledge	$0 70
Reid, M.	Caspar the Gaucho	Routledge	$0 70
Richards, L.	Captain January	Century	$1 00
Richards, L.	Quicksilver Sue	Century	$1 00
Richardson, Major	Wacousta	Briggs	$1 50
Roberts, C. G. D.	Forge in the Forest	Briggs	$1 25
Russell, W. C.	Marooned	Rand, McNally	$1 00
Russell, W. C.	Wreck of the Grosvenor	Burt	$0 75
Saintine, X. B.	Picciola	Burt	$0 75
Sand, G.	Wings of Courage	Blackie	2s 0d
Sangster, M. E	Janet Ward	Revell	$1 50
Sangster, M. E	Winsome Womanhood	Revell	$1 25
Saunders, M	Story of the Graveleys	Page	$1 20
Saunders, M	Tilda Jane	Briggs	$1 25
Scott, M	Cruise of the Midge	Blackie	2s 0d
Scott, M	Tom Cringles' Log	Blackie	2s 0d
Scott, Sir Walter	Talisman	Macmillan	$0 70
Scott, Sir Walter	Ivanhoe	Macmillan	$1 00
Scott, Sir Walter	Rob Roy	Macmillan	$1 00
Scott, Sir Walter	Old Mortality	Macmillan	$1 00
Scott, Sir Walter	Guy Mannering	Macmillan	$1 00
Scott, Sir Walter	Waverley	Macmillan	$1 00
Segur, de M	Sophie	Heath	$0 20
Sharp, E	Other Boy	Macmillan	$1 25
Sharp, E	Youngest Girl in the School	Macmillan	$1 50
Shaw, F. L	Castle Blair	Little	$1 00
Sheard, V	Trevellyan's Little Daughter	Briggs	$1 25
Smeaton, O.	Mystery of the Pacific	Blackie	3s 0d
Smith, G	Roggie and Reggie Stories	Harper	$1 50
Squire, C	Great Khans Treasure	Scribner	$1 25
Stables, Gordon	Naval Cadet	Blackie	3s 6d
Stables, Gordon	Westward with Columbus	Scribner	$1 50
Stables, Gordon	For Life and Liberty	Scribner	$1 50
Stables, Gordon	Hearts of Oak	Scribner	$1 50
Stables, Gordon	To Greenland and the Pole	Scribner	$1 50
Stables, Gordon	In the Great White Land	Blackie	3s 6d
Stables, Gordon	In Quest of the Giant Sloth	Blackie	3s 6d
Stables, Gordon	Twixt School and College	Blackie	3s 0d
Stebbing, G	That Aggravating School-girl	Nisbet	$0 75

Author.	Title.	Publisher.	Price.
Stevenson, R. L	Kidnapped	Scribner	$1 50
Stevenson, R. L	Treasure Island	Scribner	$1 50
Stockton, F. R	Jolly Fellowship	Scribner	$1 50
Stockton, F. R	Tales Out of School	Scribner	$1 50
Stockton, F. R	Clocks of Rondaine	Scribner	$1 50
Stoddard, W. O	Talking Leaves	Harper	$0 60
Stoddard, W. O	Swordsman's Son	Century	$1 50
Stoddard, W. O	With the Black Prince	Appleton	$1 50
Stowe, H. B	Dred	Various ed.	
Stowe, H. B	Uncle Tom's Cabin	Various ed.	
Stowe, H. B	Pearl of Orr's Island	Various ed.	
St. Pierre, B	Paul and Virginia	Altemus	$0 50
Strang, H	Kobo	Briggs	$1 50
Strang, H	Tom Burnaby	Briggs	$1 50
Strang, H	Boys of the Light Brigade	Briggs	$1 50
Stirling, A. H	Reign of Princess Naska	Blackie	2s 6d
Stretton, H	Hester Morley's Promise	Dodd	$1 00
Stringer, A	Lonely O'Malley	Houghton	$1 50
Stronach, A	A Newnham Friendship	Blackie	3s 6d
Stuart, R. McH	Sonny	Century	$1 00
Swan, Annie	Carlowrie	Briggs	$0 75
Swan, Annie	St. Vedas	Briggs	$1 00
Swan, Annie	Briar and Palm	Briggs	$1 00
Swan, Annie	Aldersyde	Briggs	$0 75
Swan, Annie	Sheila	Briggs	$1 00
Swan, Annie	Maitland of Lauriston	Briggs	$1 00
Thompson, L	Winning of the Victoria Cross	Caldwell	$0 75
Thomson, E. W	Walter Gibbs	Briggs	$1 25
Thomson, E. W	Old Man Savarin	Briggs	$1 00
Traill, C. P	Cot and Cradle Stories	Briggs	$1 00
Twain, Mark	Tom Sawyer	Harper	$1 75
Twain, Mark	Huckleberry Finn	Harper	$1 75
Twain, Mark	Prince and Pauper	Harper	$1 75
Twain, Mark	Innocents Abroad	Harper	$1 75
Twain, Mark	Roughing It	Harper	$1 75
Tynan, K	A Girl of Galway	Blackie	6s 0d
Tynan, K	Handsome Brandons	Blackie	3s 6d
Tytler, S	A Loyal Little Maid	Blackie	2s 6d
Tytler, S	Queen Charlotte's Maidens	Blackie	2s 0d
Tytler, S	Girl Neighbors	Blackie	3s 0d
Vachell	The Hill	Dodd	$1 50
Von Wyss	Swiss Family Robinson	Burt	$0 75
Verne, Jules	Around the Moon	Burt	$0 75
Verne, Jules	Around the World in Eighty Days	Burt	$0 75
Verne, Jules	English at the North Pole	Burt	$0 75
Verne, Jules	Twenty Thousand Leagues Under the Sea	Burt	$0 75
Wallace, Lew	Ben Hur	Harper	$1 50
Warman, Cy	White Mail	Scribners	$1 25
Weaver, Emily P	Soldiers of Liberty, a Story of the Wars in the Netherlands	Briggs	$0 35
Weber, A	For Auld Lang Syne	Briggs	$1 25
Wetherell, Miss	Queechy	Ward, Locke	$0 35
Wetherell, Miss	Wide, Wide World	Ward, Locke	$0 35
Wetherell, Miss	Melbourne House	Ward, Locke	$0 35
Wetherell, Miss	Daisy	Ward, Locke	$0 35
Wetherell, Miss	Daisy in the Field	Ward, Locke	$0 35

Author.	Title.	Publisher.	Price.
Wetherell, Miss	Ellen Montgomery's Bookshelf	Warde, Loche	$0 35
Whistler, C. W.	King Olaf's Kinsman	Blackie	3s 6d
Whistler, C. W.	Wulfric the Weapon Thane	Blackie	3s 6d
Whistler, C. W.	A Thane of Wessex	Blackie	3s 6d
Whitney, Mrs. A. D. T.	Faith Gartney's Girlhood	Houghton	$1 25
Whitney, Mrs. A. D. T.	We Girls	Houghton	$1 25
Whitney, Mrs. A. D. T.	{ A Summer in Leslie / Goldthwaite's Life }	Houghton	$1 25
Wiggin, K. D.	Birds Christmas Carol	Houghton	$0 50
Wiggin, K. D.	Story of Patsy	Houghton	$0 50
Wiggin, K. D.	Timothy's Quest	Houghton	$1 00
Wiggin, K. D.	Rebecca of Sunnybrook Farm	Briggs	$1 25
Winter, J. S.	Private Tinker	Stokes	$0 75
Wood, Mrs. H.	Orville College	Macmillan	$0 60
Wright, J. M.	Romain Kalbris	Coates	$0 75
Yonge, C. M.	Little Duke	Macmillan	$0 70
Yonge, C. M.	Daisy Chain	Macmillan	$1 00
Yonge, C. M.	Young Alcides	Macmillan	$1 00
Yonge, C. M.	Trial	Macmillan	$1 00
Yonge, C. M.	Pillars of the House	Macmillan	$2 00
York, Mrs. Eva Rose	The White Letter	Briggs	$0 50
Young, E. R., Jr.	Duck Lake	Briggs	$1 00

CPSIA information can be obtained
at www.ICGtesting.com
Printed in the USA
BVHW090629211118
533509BV00028BA/2704/P